Mrs Bootle's
Boots

by Penny Dolan

Illustrated by Maddy McClellan

W
FRANKLIN WATTS
LONDON•SYDNEY

First published in 2010 by
Franklin Watts
338 Euston Road
London
NW1 3BH

Franklin Watts Australia
Level 17/207 Kent Street
Sydney
NSW 2000

Text © Penny Dolan 2010
Illustration © Maddy McClellan 2010

A CIP catalogue record for this book is available
from the British Library.

ISBN 978 0 7496 9431 9 (hbk)
ISBN 978 0 7496 9436 4 (pbk)

Series Editor: Jackie Hamley
Series Advisor: Catherine Glavina
Series Designer: Peter Scoulding

Printed in China

Franklin Watts is a division of
Hachette Children's Books,
an Hachette UK company
www.hachette.co.uk

With thanks to St Oswald's Junior School, Guiseley – P.D.

It was home time. Ollie and Emma were waiting by the school door.

Mrs Bootle came up. "Your mum phoned," she said. "She's running late so you can wait with me."

4

Mrs Bootle was sorting out the boot box, where the lost boots were kept. "Just look," she said. "There's no name inside any of these boots."

Ollie and Emma stared.
There were old boots and
new boots, small boots and
tall boots, bright boots and
dull boots, and boots with
patterns on.

Who had left the boots at school?
Some were just dropped.

Some were left behind at
holiday times.

Some were left behind when
children went off to new schools.

They dropped the oldest boots
into a recycling bag.
"It seems a pity to get rid of these
other boots," said Emma.

"What else can we do?" replied
Mrs Bootle. "Nobody will want
to wear them."

Mum arrived. She held a tray of young plants. "Sorry I'm late, Mrs Bootle. Please have these," she said. "Put them into some pots somewhere in the school."

"But the school hasn't got any flowerpots," said Mrs Bootle.

Ollie and Emma looked at the plants, and they looked at the boots. Then they smiled. "But the school does have lots of boots," they said.

"It certainly does!" said Mrs
Bootle. "And I think tomorrow
will be a busy day for us."

Next morning, the boots were washed clean inside and out.

When the boots were dry, Emma, Ollie and their friends made them look good. Mrs Bootle put small holes in the boots.

The next day, the children filled the
boots with grit and good earth.

Then they planted tiny
plants in each boot.

Last of all, they watered
the boots well.

The children set the boot-pots in rows outside the school. Tiny green shoots peeped out of each one.

"The plants look rather
small," said Ollie.

"They'll grow soon," said Emma.

The sun shone down on the boots for some of the day. The little plants grew stronger.

Everyone took it in turns to
water the plants.

Before long, the plants grew strong
stems and leaves and buds.
Some plants climbed up
the school wall.

Then, one sunny day, the flowers
opened and spread
their bright petals.

Mrs Bootle looked very happy.
"Our school looks very cheerful
now," she said.

"Aren't you glad we had so many lost boots, Mrs Bootle?" laughed Ollie and Emma.

29

Puzzle 1

Put these pictures in the correct order.
Now try writing the story in your own words!

Puzzle 2

1. I'm sorry. I was held up at work.

2. We could use the boots as flowerpots!

3. Wait with me, children!

4. Could you plant these at school?

5. It's lucky we had the boots after all!

6. Today, class, we are making pots.

Choose the correct speech bubbles for the characters. Can you think of any others? Turn over to find the answers.

Answers

Puzzle 1

The correct order is: 1e, 2d, 3f, 4a, 5c, 6b

Puzzle 2

Mrs Bootle: 3, 6

Ollie and Emma: 2, 5

Mum: 1, 4